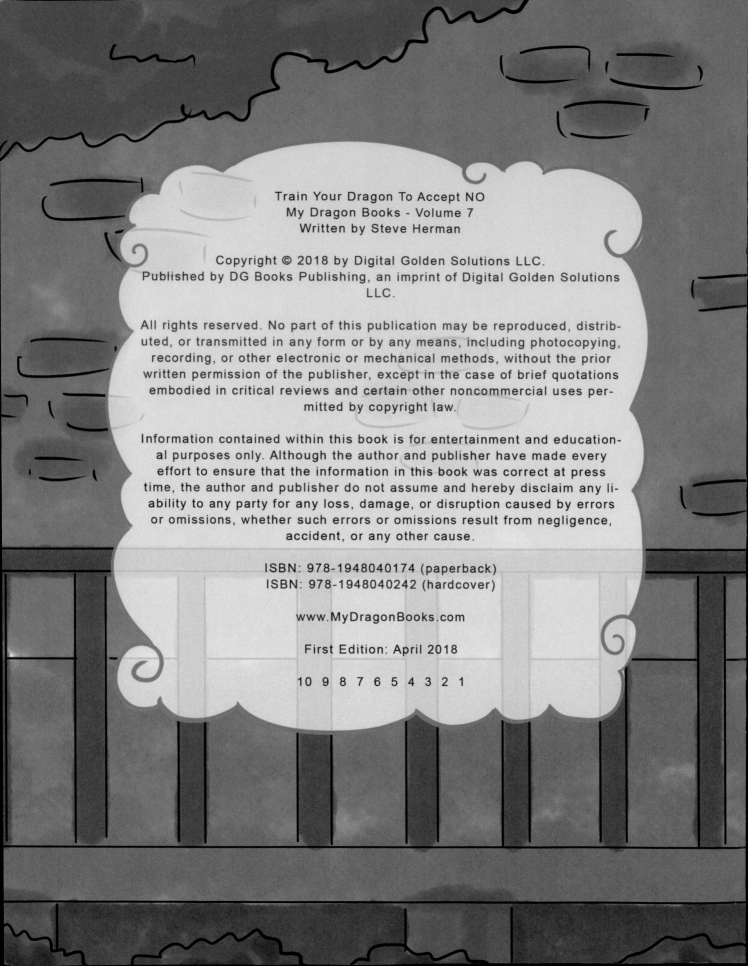

Train Your Dragon To Accept NO
My Dragon Books - Volume 7
Written by Steve Herman

ISBN: 978-1948040174 (paperback)
ISBN: 978-1948040242 (hardcover)

www.MyDragonBooks.com

First Edition: April 2018

10 9 8 7 6 5 4 3 2 1

# Train Your Dragon To Accept NO

## My Dragon Books - Volume 7

# Steve Herman

Diggory Doo's a dandy pet,
as far as dragons go...
But dragons can get really angry
when you tell them "**No!**"

But when I told him "**No,**"
Diggory Doo began to cry.

Sometimes Diggory Doo
avoided going to bed...
He asked if he could stay up late
and play some games instead.

Diggory's favorite thing to do is play out in the yard...

One day he couldn't do it;
it was raining much too hard.

Mother said to stay inside –
"No going out to play"

So Diggory threw a chair when he didn't get his way.

Diggory opened wide his mouth
and gave a mighty roar...
In his despair, he pulled my hair,
then left and slammed the door!

"Like the time I told you 'No' when you asked for chocolate pie, I wasn't being mean to you – I had a reason why."

"If you'd taken just a minute
and not behaved your worst,
You'd know that you could have
your pie – just eat your dinner first!"

"You could have heard the reason that I had to tell you '**No**' – A good night's sleep is healthy; it helps a dragon grow."

"Ask politely, 'May I borrow this,
for just a day or two?
Or trade me one of yours,
and I'll give one of mine to you!'"

Sometimes the answer's, "No, not now,"
and that's the time to learn
That dragons must be patient
as they kindly wait their turn.

When someone has to tell you **"No"**,
you should not refuse
To accept it as an answer,
remember these tricks that you can use!

They've come in very handy
for my good friend, Diggory Doo
So when you hear the word **"No"**,
perhaps you can try them, too!

Get your FREE Gift from Diggory Doo at
www.MyDragonBooks.com/gift

# Read more about Drew and Diggory Doo!

Visit
www.MyDragonBooks.com
for more!

Made in the USA
Middletown, DE
16 February 2019